WHY MENTAL-HI
LOVE PII

MW00932514

"As a psychologist, *THIS BO╌╌ ╌╌ ╌ ╌╌╌╌-READ FOR MY KID AS WELL AS YOURS.* It is up to us to introduce them to *HEROES LIKE PIPPA WHO ILLUSTRATE HOW TO FACE WHAT'S HARD & OVERCOME FEAR, ADAPT TO CHANGE, AND BEAT ANXIETY."*
— *Dr. Erica Birkley, Psychologist & Owner, Birkley Consulting*

"This generation is manifesting tremendous stress,
and struggles with anxiety are only on the rise.
The good news is anxiety issues are very treatable!
PIPPA NORMALIZES THE EXPERIENCE OF CHILDHOOD ANXIETY WHILE GIVING KIDS GREAT TOOLS TO MANAGE IT."
— *Dr. Brett Dowdy, Chief of Psychological Services,
Lindner Center of HOPE & University of Cincinnati
College of Medicine Associate Professor*

"Big feelings can be confusing for kids,
but Pippa's experiences are relatable to the
anxieties and stressors that many children face.
THE COPING SKILLS PIPPA LEARNS ARE A WONDERFUL BRIDGE FOR CHILDREN AND ADULTS TO HAVE DEEPER CONVERSATIONS about thoughts, feelings, and behaviors."
— *Dr. Natalie Thornberry, Clinical and School Counselor &
Malone University Director and Assistant Professor
of Graduate Programs in Counseling*

"As a child therapist, I see how great the need is for resources
to educate children on how to handle stress and anxiety, while
also helping them communicate their emotions in a healthy
way. *PIPPA COMBINES THIS KIND OF LEARNING WITH FUN, MAKING IT A POWERFUL RESOURCE TO HELP KIDS UNDERSTAND THEIR OWN ANXIETY AND LEARN SKILLS TO MANAGE IT!"*
— *Katie Dixon, MA, LPCC-S, Child and Family Counselor*

Dedicated to my husband and kids,
who have embraced Pippa like a part of the family
and encouraged me to "Speak Up!" with her story.

PIPPA SPEAKS UP!

Book 1 in the
*PIPPA POTTER,
PRESIDENT'S DAUGHTER*
series

Written & Illustrated
by Elizabeth James

ISBN 979-8-989-1101-0-0 (paperback)

Library of Congress Control Number: 2023918001

Published in the United States by Big Heart Books.

BIG HEART
books

Get your FREE RESOURCE GUIDE for PARENTS & TEACHERS

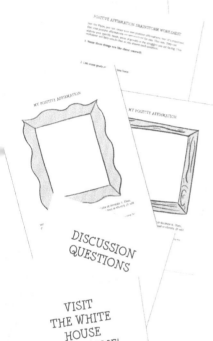

A PARENT'S GUIDE TO BODY SCANS WITH KIDS

DISCUSSION QUESTIONS

VISIT THE WHITE HOUSE FROM HOME!

PARENT & TEACHER RESOURCES
to accompany

PIPPA POTTER
PRESIDENT'S DAUGHTER

PIPPA SPEAKS UP!

WRITTEN & ILLUSTRATED BY
ELIZABETH JAMES

SIGN UP TO DOWNLOAD IT NOW:

with more than 25 pages of extra content!

MOM
(the President)

DAD
(breakfast-maker)

PIPPA
(that's me!)

OTTO
(baby brother #1)

OLLIE
(baby brother #2)

ROSIE
(nanny)

TONY
(Secret Service agent)

TALIA
(best friend)

COOPER
(annoying classmate)

DYLAN
(annoying sidekick)

PSSST...!

As you're reading, keep an eye out for icons in the margins like this one: 📖

When you see one, that lets you know that that part of the story is actually based on facts from real life! You can read more about those facts in the back of the book. (Like, if you lived in the White House, maids really could clean your room for you...if your parents would let them!)

We hope you have fun reading and learning along with Pippa!

CHAPTER 1

I make sure I don't look up from my desk. My teacher, Miss Jones, is reading questions to the class. It's supposed to be "for fun." But you never know when a teacher might call on you, just for making eye contact.

There's nothing fun about that.

Instead, I focus on an old worksheet. Around the paper's edge, I outline a spiky cluster of crystals. Crystals always make me feel better. Even when I'm just drawing them.

"Next question," Miss Jones says. "What do you call a scientist who studies rocks?"

I suck in my breath and look up. A geologist!

PIPPA LOVES ROCKS
— 3 YEARS OLD —

Of course, I know that because I've been collecting rocks since I was little.

I used to keep so many in my pockets that I broke our washing machine once. (Oops!) But Mom never forgot to check my pockets again.

Until recently. Because obviously she doesn't do our laundry anymore. Instead, a whole team of housekeepers takes care of it now.

Miss Jones continues reading. "Is it: An astronomer? A biologist? A rock star? Or, a geologist?"

I squirm in my seat. I know the answer is a geologist. I probably knew that in preschool!

The problem is that I don't know *how* to answer it. Some people don't think twice about raising their hands in class. But some people do. And I'm one of those kinds of people.

My eyes dart around the room. I want to raise my hand. I want to show Miss Jones and everyone else at Capitol Academy—especially Cooper and Dylan—that I know more than just who the President is and what she had last night for dinner. (Although, I don't even seem to know that anymore.)

My best friend, Talia, turns in her seat. She gives me a knowing smile. My fingers tremble. Then, I lift my hand...but not to answer the question.

Instead, I reach up and grab the crystal that hangs from a chain around my neck. It's cool and smooth. I rub its edges between my fingers.

Miss Jones sighs. "Scientists who study rocks are called *geologists*," she says.

Now, I'm the one who sighs. Why couldn't I just raise my hand? But it's no use. Like the rocks in my collection, I can't change how I'm made. Not even if I wanted to.

Afterward, during our restroom break, Talia skips up to me.

"I thought for sure you knew that answer," she chirps. "Since you like rocks so much."

"I did," I mumble and look away.

"What?" Talia's eyebrows scrunch together. "Then why didn't you answer it?"

"I don't know," I say. My cheeks heat up. "I

just...I just couldn't."

I race into a restroom stall before Talia can ask another question. She doesn't understand. Nothing scares her—nothing! She has a pet rat at home and a whole tub of worms.

She loves talking to people. Even strangers! Answering a question in front of the whole class is nothing to Talia. But it *is* something to me...

I wait until everyone—including Talia—leaves the restroom.

Only then do I head back to class. The hallway is almost empty.

Except for Tony, the Secret Service agent who follows me everywhere. It's his job to keep me safe.

And, except for Cooper and Dylan.

For some reason, they seem to follow me everywhere, too. Even though it's definitely not their job.

HIS JOB TO FOLLOW ME AROUND...

"Hey, Prez!" Cooper hollers from behind me.

I haven't been at Capitol Academy for very long, but I already know to stay away from them both. All I want is to blend in here.

But Cooper and Dylan won't let that happen. They always find ways to remind everyone that my mom's the President of the United States. As if anyone could forget—no one else here is followed around by a Secret Service agent!

I walk faster and pretend I don't hear them both snickering.

Back in class, it's time for language arts.

"We're going to start a new class project," Miss Jones announces.

Cooper groans. Dylan mutters something. Miss Jones ignores them both.

"Don't worry," she says, smiling. "This is going to be a lot of fun!"

Back home, my favorite projects involved field trips and having class outside. I lean forward, wondering what special projects are like here at Capitol Academy.

Then Miss Jones explains, "We're going to give class speeches!"

I gasp, dropping the pencil I'm holding. The pencil rolls off my desk and lands on the floor with a *plink!*

When Miss Jones finishes explaining the project, she's still smiling. "Isn't this going to be so much fun?"

Only Talia grins back.

I scramble to pick up my pencil. Then I reach up and squeeze my necklace. There's definitely nothing fun about this. Nothing at all!

CHAPTER 2

After school, I wait with Talia in the cafeteria until she's picked up. She's been my best friend since I started at Capitol Academy. That was only a couple months ago.

Before then, I went to school in Ohio. No one there cared what my mom's job was. But once I moved here, Talia was the only one who *didn't* care that my mom was the President. Which is why she's more than just my best friend at Capitol Academy. She's pretty much my only friend here.

"I can't wait to start on my speech," Talia says. "I already decided on my topic. I'm going to talk about my worms!"

TALIA
(SHE ISN'T AFRAID OF ANYTHING!)

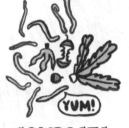

COMPOSTS
WITH WORMS

ALWAYS
RAISES HER
HAND

COLLECTS WORM
POOP!

PET RAT,
REMINGTON

LOVES TO GARDEN

Those would be the worms she uses for composting. I already know all about them: They live in a big container in her laundry room, where Talia feeds them leftover fruits and vegetables. Over time, they eat through the scraps. As they do, they leave behind poop. Talia scoops it out and uses it in her garden. Which I also already know all about.

"What will you do your speech on?" Talia asks.

I don't want to think about that. So I shrug instead.

"You can use one of my ideas," Talia beams. "I came up with extras."

Talia lists some. Like how to grow tomatoes or collect rain for watering plants.

"You could also do your speech about Remington," she says. Remington is her pet rat. "He can use the toilet!"

I shudder. But not because she's talking about a rat. I don't want to do a speech on *anything*. Fortunately, Talia doesn't notice. Because that's when her dad's big green van drives up.

I sniff the air and smile. He owns a vegetarian restaurant called The Green Café. He re-uses its cooking oil to fuel his van. Which makes the air

smell like French fries wherever he drives!

I wave goodbye as Talia leaves.

Then, Tony and I walk back through the school. His shoes make loud, squeaky noises with each step. But other than that, the halls—including both of us—are quiet.

We exit through a side door. The Secret Service decided this was safer than using the front doors like everyone else. They decide what's safe and not safe about *everything* I do.

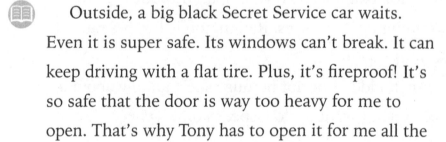

Outside, a big black Secret Service car waits. Even it is super safe. Its windows can't break. It can keep driving with a flat tire. Plus, it's fireproof! It's so safe that the door is way too heavy for me to open. That's why Tony has to open it for me all the time.

Once he does, Rosie is already inside the car. I slide in beside her. Back in Ohio, she was our nanny. When we moved to the White House, Rosie came with us.

"Can we go to the museum?" I ask, rubbing my crystal necklace. I'm talking about the Smithsonian National Museum of Natural History. It has one of the biggest rock collections in the world, with crystals and gems in every color of the rainbow. Ever since moving here, it's where I go when I need to feel better. Like now, with the speech at school.

"The Secret Service has to approve things like that first," Rosie says. "I don't think they can arrange that on such short notice."

My shoulders slump. The Secret Service always has something to say about what I can and can't do. Mostly, about what I *can't* do.

"How was school?" Rosie asks. I know she's just changing the subject.

"Fine." I look out the window. I don't want to think about the speech, much less talk about it.

"Guess what's for dessert tonight?" Rosie grins and playfully nudges my side.

I can't help but smile back as we answer together, "Buckeyes!"

Buckeyes are my favorite, chocolate-covered treats. They remind me of home. My real home, back in Ohio. Where me and Mom used to make them together.

But now the head pastry chef at the White House makes them instead.

I cross my fingers. "Will Mom be there?"

Rosie shakes her head. "No, she's eating in the West Wing tonight."

I sigh. That's what I was afraid of. The West Wing is where her office is. It's in a separate building next to the White House. Mom seems to spend more and more time there lately.

Tony holds his wrist up to his mouth and talks into the microphone attached to it. "Crystal has arrived." He's talking about me. My whole family has code names that start with the letter "C." I go by "Crystal." Mom is known as "Compassion," and Dad got "Curiosity." My little brothers, Otto and

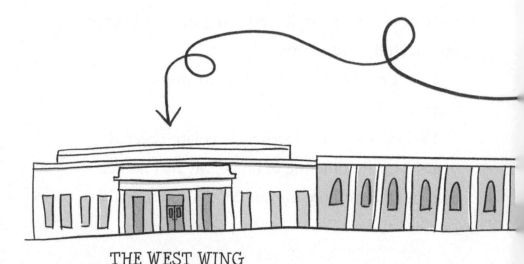

THE WEST WING

OUR SECRET CODE NAMES

CRYSTAL COMPASSION

CURIOSITY COOKIE CAKE

Ollie, are called "Cake" and "Cookie."

We pull up to the White House. Tony opens the car door, and I climb out. Past some bushes and trees, I can see the West Wing. Mom has never worked this close to home before. But she seems farther away than ever.

THE WHITE HOUSE

CHAPTER 3

Being at home after school is a lot different now that I live in the White House. Back in Ohio, it was just me, my brothers and Rosie until my parents got home from work. Then, when Rosie left, it was just us Potters.

But now, there are *always* people in the White House. Besides having Tony with me everywhere I go *outside* the house, I'm never alone *inside* the house, either.

 Complete strangers walk through here every day! Tours take them through the downstairs part of the house. Thankfully, they can't come upstairs to the Residence, where we live.

But there are still lots of people up here. Almost a hundred people work here in the Residence! They do everything from make us food to fix the lights and clean the toilets. (They *could* make my bed and clean my room for me. But Mom won't let them. She says it's important that I learn "responsibility.")

Once I'm inside the White House, I race upstairs. The Residence takes up the second and third floors of the house. It's the only part that feels like home. That's because downstairs is like a museum for the tours. We can't change anything down there. But upstairs, we can. We even got to hire a decorator to help!

But I didn't want the decorator's help. I wanted my room to feel like *my room*. So I brought as much stuff from home as I could. Which Mom couldn't argue with because my new room is huge! I brought my bean bag chair and the blankets on my bed and every one of my pillows.

Of course, I also brought my rock collection. Back home, I had to keep it in different plastic cases. But here, I have the perfect place for it. Rows and rows of shelves are built right into the walls. I spread my rocks out along each one. Then, I added

tags about each rock and where it was from. It almost feels like my own museum every time I walk in.

I grab my *Rock Collector's Guidebook*. When most people think of collecting rocks, they think of gold and diamonds. But not me. My favorite rocks are quartz crystals.

Quartz is a pretty common mineral, so it isn't worth much. But what makes it my favorite is how many colors it can be. It can be red, orange, yellow, green, blue, purple, pink, gray, brown, black or white. It can also have multiple colors mixed together.

I look at the crystal on my necklace. It's also a quartz, but it's the white kind. The only one I still don't have in my collection is the yellow color, citrine. It's the rarest kind of quartz.

I open my guidebook to the pages about citrine. It says that thousands of years ago, people believed citrine gave you good luck.

Too bad I don't have any citrine. Because I could use some good luck. Like with spending more time with my mom. Or with Capitol Academy and the kids there. And definitely with my speech.

But since I don't, I try not to think about any of
that at all. At least, not until I have to…

The next morning, I wake up to
the sweet smell of pancakes. I
climb out of bed and follow the
scent to the Residence kitchen,
where Dad is at the stove. This is
one change about the White
House that I do like.

That's because when we moved here, Dad quit
his job as a therapist. He said he wanted to spend
more time together as a family. Mostly that means
taking care of my twin brothers, Otto and Ollie. But
it also means making us breakfast each morning.

"Good morning, Pippa!" Dad says. "Will it be one
pancake or two?"

"Just one, please." I sit down across from Otto
and Ollie. They're in booster seats, eating pancakes
with their hands. I guess when you're only two,
there's nothing wrong with that.

Down the hall, I hear a *click-click-click!*

"Mom!" I squeal at the sound of her shoes on the

floor. As soon as she steps into the kitchen, my arms fly around her waist. Even though it's first thing in the morning, she's already dressed in a scratchy suit.

Dad turns and bows in front of Mom. "Would the President of the United States like one of my world-famous pancakes?"

"Please stop bowing like that, Mitchell," Mom says, chuckling at Dad. "You look silly. Besides, I don't have time for breakfast. I have a meeting."

Of course, she has a meeting.

She kisses Otto and Ollie goodbye before leaving the kitchen. She's heads to the West Wing, and then, she's gone.

I sigh and pick up my fork. But I can't take another bite. The thought of sticky-sweet pancakes makes my stomach churn.

Instead, I go back to my room to get ready. My guidebook is still open to the page about citrine. I frown and slam the book closed. Because, lately, Mom seems about as rare around here as citrine. Except without the good luck.

CHAPTER 4

At school a few days later, Miss Jones tells us to get our computers out.

"We're going to work on your speeches," she says.

I gulp. Usually, I have my assignments done ahead of time. Usually, I even turn them in early. But not this one. Every time I try, all I can think about is standing up in front of everyone. Then, I think about how everyone will stare at me. More than they already do.

"What if we haven't picked a topic yet?" Dylan asks.

"Come on!" Cooper says. "I thought you were doing LeBron James?"

"It's fine, Dylan," Miss Jones says. "But please pick one by Monday morning. Maybe hearing other people's ideas will help those of you who haven't decided. Would anyone like to share their topic?"

Kids raise their hands. It doesn't take me long to realize that me and Dylan are the only ones who *haven't* picked our topics. I slump in my seat and hope Miss Jones doesn't notice that I haven't raised my hand.

One student says her speech is going to be on Abraham Lincoln.

Cooper perks up. "Wasn't he a President?"

"Yes, he was," Miss Jones says. "I'm sure it will make for a fascinating speech."

"Whoa," Cooper screeches. "What if Prez does hers on the *current* President? That's not fair. She can't do a speech on her own mom!"

Some kids turn around and look at me. Others start whispering and murmuring.

My face burns. I would never do an assignment about my mom! I want to say that out loud. But the words catch in my throat. Instead, I fumble with the crystal around my neck, wishing more than ever that it was a good luck charm.

"That's enough," Miss Jones says. "It sounds like most of you are off to a great start. Let's get back to our research. Please, open your computers and get started."

Fortunately, everyone obeys. Except me. My mind is still swirling from what just happened. So I bury my head in my arms on my desk. It's dark in there, almost like I'm one of my crystals, buried deep underground. I almost forget I'm still in class.

Until Miss Jones leans down beside me. "Pippa, are you feeling okay?"

I sit straight up, and my cheeks flush pink again.

"I'm fine," I say, opening my computer. "I'm totally fine."

Then I hear mumbling from the back corner of the room. But it isn't mumbling like the kind Cooper and Dylan do. It's the grown-up kind of mumbling. Then I hear my code name, "Crystal." I turn around. It's Tony in the back of the room, talking into his wrist microphone.

He marches to the front of the room and whispers to Miss Jones. She dismisses us for a restroom break. I've never been happier to leave class, so I rush out as fast as I can.

"Pippa!" Talia calls from behind me. I stop to walk with her, but Tony is right behind me.

"Follow me," he says, leading me away from the restrooms.

Talia calls out, "Where are you going?"

But I don't know. I shake my head and race to keep up with Tony. When we burst out the side doors, the Secret Service car is there.

"What's going on?" I ask.

"We need to leave," he says, opening the door to the backseat.

I climb in and buckle up, but I'm still confused. School isn't over! We left so suddenly that Rosie isn't even here.

Then it hits me: Why we had to leave so quickly...

"Did something happen to Mom? Is she okay?"

Tony looks at me from the rearview mirror.

"Compassion is fine," he says, using Mom's code name. He pauses for a moment. Then he takes a deep breath and puts on his sunglasses. "It's you I'm worried about."

CHAPTER 5

"But why?" I cry, as the car pulls away from Capitol Academy. "I feel fine!"

Tony is speaking into his microphone and doesn't answer.

This doesn't make any sense at all. Why did I have to leave in the middle of the day? The only time I've ever left school halfway through was for a doctor's or dentist's appointment or if I was sick.

Wait a minute...

I lean forward in my seat as I piece together what's happening. "Did we leave because I laid my head down?"

Tony peers over the top edge of his sunglasses.

"I've arranged for you to see the White House

doctor," he says.

I was right!

"But I'm fine," I squeak. I feel like I could cry.

"The doctor will check you out to make sure," Tony says. He doesn't even look in the rearview mirror.

I fling myself back against the seat and look out the window. I can't believe I have to go to a doctor for this. All I did was lay my head down on my desk! This never would have happened if my mom wasn't the President.

When we get to the White House, Rosie is waiting for me. Tony opens the door, but I refuse to look at him. Instead, I stomp past.

Rosie leads me to the basement of the White House. In my old house back in Ohio, our basement was full of cardboard boxes, Christmas decorations and our washing machine and dryer. The White

House basement, though, is like its own little village. It has its own paint shop, carpentry shop, flower shop, chocolate shop and even a bowling alley down there! Plus dozens more rooms and offices. Including dentist's and doctor's offices, too.

THE WHITE HOUSE BASEMENT

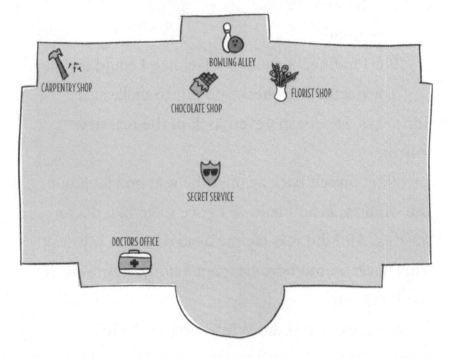

BOWLING ALLEY

CARPENTRY SHOP

CHOCOLATE SHOP

FLORIST SHOP

SECRET SERVICE

DOCTORS OFFICE

When we arrive, a young doctor with short hair is waiting.

"Pippa, this is Doctor Easton," Rosie says. "She's part of the medical unit here at the White House."

Rosie leaves, closing the door behind her. I look

around the room. Our doctor's office back home always had pictures of animals on the walls: There was one of waddling penguins and another of lion cubs playing together. My favorite was the mama elephant and her baby elephant. But in here, there isn't a single poster.

Doctor Easton points me to the exam table, where I climb up and sit. She sits in the rolling chair, which looks a lot more comfortable than this table.

"Let's talk about what's going on." She looks over her notes. "I hear you weren't feeling well at school today?"

"I'm fine," I tell her. Just like I told Miss Jones and Tony. And Rosie when she asked, too. But no one seems to believe me.

Doctor Easton smiles. "Sometimes we don't realize how our bodies are actually feeling. Why don't you think about it for a minute? Then, let me know."

Doctor Easton starts working on some papers. I don't know what else to do, so I close my eyes. The room is cool and quiet as I sit still on the table.

I start at the top of my head and try to pay

attention to each body part, one at a time. First my forehead, then on down to my chin, neck and shoulders.

That's when I feel it.

"It feels like my heart is beating really fast," I tell her. I never noticed that before. "And my stomach feels kind of twisted."

"Great job listening to your body!" Doctor Easton grabs her stethoscope. "Now, let's see what's going on."

She listens to my heartbeat, presses on my stomach, and asks me about what I ate.

"Well, I have some good news," Doctor Easton says afterward, setting her chart down on her desk. "I don't think you're sick. But it's important to pay attention to how your body is feeling. Don't be afraid to speak up if you need some help. We're here to help you! How you're feeling matters."

Doctor Easton smiles as she opens the door. I race outside, where Rosie is waiting for me.

"How was it?" she asks.

"Fine," I answer. Then I gulp. Because maybe everything isn't as fine as I'd thought.

CHAPTER 6

Rosie and I are still outside the doctor's office when I start to feel…well, I don't know how I feel. The doctor told me to think about it, but I don't want to. I just want to feel better. There's only one way to do that.

"Rosie, I need to go to the museum." I clench my hands at my side before adding, *"Now."*

I can't believe I said that out loud! My chest puffs out as I wait for Rosie to answer.

But when she looks up from her tablet, Rosie says, "Pippa, you know we have to clear these things with the Secret Service first." She smiles but looks back down at her tablet again. "I'll see if we can get something on the schedule for next week."

I groan. I can't wait that long! But Rosie already has her calendar page open and is tapping on the screen.

Then, a voice booms from behind us. "Actually, I think we can make that work today." Rosie and I both turn to face Tony. I forgot the Secret Service has an office down here in the White House basement, too.

He leads us to the Secret Service car. I'm glad I get to go to the museum after all. But I still cross my arms the whole way there.

When we get to the Smithsonian, we go upstairs to the second floor. That's where they keep the national gem collection. It's in a section called the Hall of Geology, Gems, and Minerals.

I can't get up there fast enough.

Rosie waits outside the exhibit so she can work on her tablet. Too bad Tony doesn't have any work

SMITHSONIAN MUSEUM OF NATURAL HISTORY

like that. His work is the same as always: follow me around wherever I go.

The most famous artifact here is displayed right at the entrance: the Hope Diamond. It's a giant blue diamond surrounded by lots of smaller diamonds. Tourists love to crowd around it and gawk. But not me. I march right past it. That's not what I'm here for.

I stomp until I make my way to where the rooms darken. The only lights in this section are over the rocks themselves, which are displayed in glass cases lining every wall. I love how the museum displays a lot of them by color. It's like I'm inside a rainbow cave or something. Usually that's enough to make me feel better.

But not today. Today, even my rocks don't help. I try reading some of the signs inside the cases. One is about how minerals can form when hot, molten magma from deep within the earth cools down under intense pressure over a long period of time.

But the words feel jumbled, so I keep walking. I even walk past my favorite part, the rainbow quartz

case. It has huge quartz crystals in all different colors, from white to purple to deep, dark gray. That's where you can also find the yellow citrine.

"I thought those were your favorites," a voice behind me says.

I jump and twirl around. It's Tony. I forgot he was still with me—that he's always with me. But I didn't forget that I'm upset at him. I feel like the hot, molten magma from the sign. Except that I haven't cooled down yet! Before I know it, the words spew out of me like lava.

"Why did you do it?" I cross my arms.

"What do you mean?" Tony asks. "Usually, you look at the quartz ones for a long time."

I didn't know he knew that. But that's not what I meant.

"No, why did you make me see the doctor?"

Tony sighs. "My job is to pay attention to things and keep you safe. Today, you looked like you were getting sick in class. You didn't want to say anything, but I have to. How you're feeling matters."

For the first time since we left school, I look up at Tony. He shrugs and gives me a smile. Maybe he really was trying to help.

I let out a big breath and realize that I don't feel like boiling magma anymore. I can feel myself cooling down. Maybe that's how crystals feel when they start to form...

Then Tony points back to the case I just passed.

"Do you want to go back and look at them again? I know how much you like the yellow ones, especially."

"Citrine," I beam. "The yellow ones are called citrine. They're the rarest kind of quartz."

When we get to the display, he asks me about the other colors. I tell him that the purple quartz are called amethyst and the dark ones are smoky quartz. We continue through the exhibit. Sometimes he asks questions, and sometimes I just tell him facts I know. Sometimes, we just walk in silence like we normally do.

Finally, we get to where the lights become bright again. We walk through the rest of the wing before exiting into a sunny hallway. It's like a jungle, filled with lush plants and trees. It always makes me feel like I just went on a real adventure. Especially today!

On the way back to find Rosie, Tony says, "I'm

glad you said something."

"About what?" I ask.

"About wanting to come to the museum. Even about what was upsetting you." He winks before putting his sunglasses back on. I grin. Because I'm glad I said something, too.

DO YOU LIKE PIPPA?!

If so, we would love for you to ask your parent if you can leave a short review for it online. Reviews like yours can help other kids find out about Pippa and this book!

Visit www.elizabethjameswrites.com/review or scan this QR to get links to leave a review:

WHAT CAN YOU SAY IN A REVIEW?

Anything you want! Here are a few things you could share when you write yours:

- What do you like about Pippa?
- What has been the most exciting part so far?
- Did you learn anything interesting yet?

THANKS SO MUCH! You can also share your review on social media and use #PippaPotter so we can find and share it as well!

CHAPTER 7

When we return to the Residence, Rosie and I go upstairs to the Solarium. It's on the third floor with huge windows that overlook the city. Dad turned it into a playroom for Otto and Ollie, so there's a tent in one corner and a sandbox in another.

Otto and Ollie are in the sandbox playing. I sit down and scoop up some sand, too. Then, I notice Dad and Rosie whispering together. Whispering is never good.

"What's going on?" I ask.

They look at each other, but neither says anything.

Finally, Dad shrugs. "Mom had to go on an

emergency trip. There was a hurricane."

"Where?" I ask.

"Madagascar," Rosie answers. "In Africa."

My head drops. That's way farther than the West Wing. That's the other side of the world! I never see Mom as it is. Now, it feels like I never will.

"Your mom really wants them to know that our country cares about them," Dad says.

But doesn't she care about me, too? She didn't even say goodbye! I want to say something, but I know it won't change anything. She's probably already over the ocean somewhere.

"Maybe you can invite Talia over," Dad suggests. "Wouldn't that be fun?"

It would. But it would be more fun if it wasn't only because Mom is gone…again.

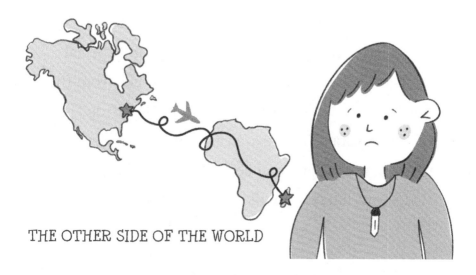

THE OTHER SIDE OF THE WORLD

It feels like forever, but Talia finally arrives at the White House on Saturday afternoon. She's the first friend to ever visit me here, if you don't count Rosie. Which I don't, since it's her job to be here.

Tony brings Talia up to the Residence in the family elevator. When the elevator doors open, Talia is grinning.

"Pippa, this is incredible," she squeals. "You never told me you had an elevator!"

I giggle. "Actually, there are *three*. But this is the main one we use."

I lead Talia to my bedroom. On the way, she looks at everything: She laughs at the serious faces in the paintings on the walls. She admires the huge vases of flowers on every table. She stands still like a statue every time a housekeeper or butler walks by.

I can't wait to show her my rock collection. Including some that I've been saving for a special occasion: They look just like normal rocks from the outside. But I'm pretty sure that on the inside are hidden crystals! Those are called geodes. I can't wait to crack them open and see!

I show Talia the geodes and tell her my plan.

"I bet we can get hammers from the carpentry shop in the basement," I say.

"You have a *what* in your basement?" Talia exclaims. Her eyes glitter like the crystals that I know are inside those rocks. "What else is down there?"

I list off some of the places, and she grabs my arm.

"A flower shop? In your house?" She marches us toward the elevator. "I can't wait to tell my dad about this!"

Downstairs, we peek inside the flower shop. Buckets and buckets of different flowers fill the room. Talia admires them all until it's time to go to the carpentry shop.

But as we exit the flower shop, Talia spots the bowling alley. It's only a couple doors down. The carpentry shop, though, is in the back corner of the basement. Why does it have to be so far away?

"Let's go bowling!" Talia says, dragging me inside.

I figure we can still get the hammers after we bowl one game. But when we finish, Talia's ready for dinner. Especially after finding out that the White

House chefs will make us anything we want.

"Anything at all?" Talia asks. Her dad is a great cook. But at home, they usually just eat leftovers from his restaurant.

As I wait for Talia to finish eating, I look out the window. The sun is starting to set. If we hurry, we can still smash open the geodes before it gets too dark outside.

But when Talia finishes, she asks, "What's next?

Should we check out the chocolate shop for dessert?"

Time is running out!

I squeeze my eyes closed. When I needed to go to the museum, I spoke up and it worked. Maybe it will work again, now.

"Let's get the hammers first." I'm surprised how strong my voice sounds. "Before it gets too late."

Talia agrees, and we go back downstairs. We walk past the bowling alley and the flower shop. But when we get to the carpentry shop, the door doesn't budge. They already locked up for the evening!

Talia shrugs. "Should we check out the chocolate shop instead?"

She skips down the hall, but I don't. If only we had gone to the carpentry shop earlier! We could have gotten the hammers and opened the rocks already. I've been saving them for so long…

But Talia doesn't notice. Because when I finally reach the chocolate shop, she grabs both my hands. "I can't wait to tell my dad about this!"

CHAPTER 8

But Talia doesn't just tell her dad. By Monday morning, everyone enters class talking about food and drinks and desserts.

"Just snap your fingers, and someone will bring you any food you want," one girl says.

I assume they're talking about some fancy new restaurant. One kid's dad writes about restaurants for a local magazine. Talia's dad owns one, and a lot of the others eat out every meal. So, it doesn't seem weird. At least not at first.

Then, Cooper comes over to my desk.

"When do I get to come over, Prez?"

"W-what?" I stammer. I have no clue what he's

talking about.

"When do I get to come over to your house?" He looks back at Dylan and laughs. "I already know what I'm going to order: one of those big turkey legs like you get at the fair. Maybe a steak and some ribs, too. And I've always wondered what crème brûlée tastes like, so maybe I'd order one of those just to see."

Suddenly, I realize he's talking about my house. My face turns red, and I clench my fists. Thoughts race through my head. I sputter, unsure of what to say. Then it's too late, because he's already back at his seat.

That's when Talia skips into the room. Finally, I understand what's going on. Talia waves to me as she slides into her seat. But I don't wave back. Because now I know: Everyone is talking about the chefs and the food and my house because of *her*.

When it's time for language arts, Miss Jones tells us to work on our speeches.

Talia turns around to show me the poster she's working on. She's drawing the different kinds of food her composting worms can and cannot eat. But I pretend like I don't see her.

Instead, I tap on my computer keyboard. Like I'm actually doing something. But I'm not.

All that's in front of me is a blank computer screen. I still haven't picked my idea yet. With Mom gone and Talia over, I totally forgot to think about a topic over the weekend. Now, with everyone talking about eating at my house, I can't think at all.

"Great work, everyone," Miss Jones says from the front of the class. "Today, we'll pick time slots for when each of you will deliver your speech. Who wants to go first?"

The class groans.

Talia raises her hand. "My dad's restaurant is

closed on Tuesdays. Is it okay if I go then so he can come?"

I frown. Of course, she doesn't have a problem volunteering! Too bad the speeches start on Monday. I feel Talia turn around and face me, but I continue to stare at my blank computer screen.

Miss Jones writes Talia's name down for Tuesday. Then she asks the class, "Who wants to go first on Monday?"

Cooper grumbles. "What about Prez? Her mom gives speeches for a living. She should go first!"

My body stiffens. Why does he always pick on me? First, he says all those things about my house. Now this? And why can't he just call me by my name? It's not like "Pippa" is hard to say.

But instead of saying anything back, I grip my crystal and begin zipping it back and forth across the chain.

Zip. Zip. Maybe Miss Jones didn't hear him. Or if she did, maybe she'll tell him to be quiet and leave me alone.

"That's a great idea," Miss Jones says. "Pippa, I'm sure you already know a ton about giving speeches from your mom. You can show the class how it's done!"

I freeze. This must be a dream! But I know it's not. I begin zipping my crystal back and forth faster.

Zip, zip. Why does it matter who my mom is? Just because she loves talking in front of crowds doesn't mean I do, too.

Zip, zip. Then I remember I haven't even started my project yet. My heart pounds. There's no way I can go first!

Thoughts whiz through my head. I chew my lip as I zip the crystal back and forth. *Zip, zip, zip.*

Snap!

In an instant, the chain breaks. It dangles from my fist. My eyes fill with tears, and I want to lay my head down on my

desk.

But I can't. Last time I did that, I ended up in the doctor's office.

Suddenly, I remember that Doctor Easton told me to pay attention to what my body was feeling. I close my eyes. I focus on the top of my head and what I feel there. I move down to my face, my neck, my shoulders. Then, I notice my heart thumping. There's also that twisted-up feeling in my stomach again.

Another thing Doctor Easton said rings in my ears: "Don't be afraid to speak up if you need some help. We're here to help you."

That's when I decide to do something I've never done before. I raise my hand.

"I need to see the doctor," I say when Miss Jones calls on me. Talia looks back at me with a worried look, but I focus on gathering my backpack.

Tony mumbles into his wrist. Before I know it, we're out the classroom, down the hallway and back inside the Secret Service car. I slump in my seat and lean my head against the window.

"Don't worry," Tony says, looking back in the rearview mirror. "We'll make sure you're okay. I'm

64

glad you said something this time."

"Thanks," I whisper. I pull the crystal from my pocket where I had put it after the chain broke. I rub it in between my fingers.

Then I add, "Me, too."

CHAPTER 9

Once I'm home, I visit Doctor Easton. Then Rosie
takes me back to my room. It's not long before
there's a knock on my door.

"Come in," I say from my bed.

When the door opens, Dad walks in.

"Dad!" I didn't think he'd find out about this. My
heart races. Maybe I made a mistake leaving school,
after all…

Dad gives me a smile as he sits on my bed.
"You're not in trouble, Pippa."

"Really?" I breathe out a big sigh of relief.

"Really." Then he asks me about what's been
going on.

Suddenly, it all spills out: About class and the speech and how Doctor Easton told me to pay attention to my body. I tell him about the twisted-up feeling and asking to see the doctor.

"It sounds like your body is trying to tell you something," Dad says.

"What do you mean?" I ask. "Doctor Easton said I'm not sick."

"Our bodies can tell us that we're sick when we have a runny nose or a cough," Dad says. "But they can also tell us other things, too. Like how we're feeling, emotionally."

"How?" I ask.

"Well, it sounds to me like your body is telling you it's scared," Dad says. "Does that sound right?"

I look down at my blanket and nod.

"That's totally normal to feel scared about things like giving a speech at school," Dad says. "Sometimes those feelings can even be a good thing, like if they help you finish the project."

"But I haven't started it yet," I whisper. I reach up to squeeze my crystal, forgetting that it's not around my neck anymore.

"Then it sounds like your body needs help

calming down," Dad says. "That's why it's good you're paying attention to how you're feeling. That's the first step. And it can be the hardest part."

Then I think of something.

"What about how I always rub my crystal necklace? Is that my body talking to me, too?"

"It could be," Dad says. "Our bodies will try to get our attention in different ways. Once you recognize what those are, you can help your body calm down. That's the next step."

"How do you do that?"

"You might have to try different ones to see what works best for you," Dad says. "You can take long, deep breaths. Or talk about your feelings with someone you trust. Or encourage yourself with positive statements. Those can all work together to help your body calm down."

Just then, someone else knocks on my door. It swings open.

"Mom!" I squeal. She plops down on my bed and gives me a hug.

"I didn't know you were back!" I snuggle against her.

"We just landed," she says.

"Perfect timing!" Dad winks one eye at Mom. "Because we were just talking about calming our bodies down. Like when someone has to give a speech."

"I guess I did come at the right time," Mom says with a chuckle. "Because, I *still* have to help calm my body down whenever I give a speech."

"You do?" I can't believe it. I thought she loved giving speeches. Especially when everyone stands up and claps at the end.

Mom nods. "But it's gotten better since your dad helped me learn to calm myself down beforehand."

Mom shows me how she closes her eyes and takes deep breaths. She points to her belly, and tells me to watch how it fills up like a balloon when she breathes in. That's why she calls it her "balloon breathing."

Then she tells me it's my turn. I feel silly, but Mom and Dad don't laugh, so I close my eyes and copy them. I breathe in as slowly as I can, making my belly puff out. Then, I breathe out just as slowly. We do it over and over again.

Afterward, we brainstorm some positive things I can tell myself when I'm feeling scared. My favorite

EVERYTHING WILL BE OKAY—NO MATTER WHAT HAPPENS NEXT.

ones are, "I can be brave," and, "Everything will be okay—no matter what happens next."

"How are you feeling now?" Dad asks.

I take a moment to think. Then I grin. "Fine!" This time, I mean it. Maybe those things really helped, after all.

Then I remember something else…

"I haven't even started my speech yet," I cry. "I don't know what to do it on!"

Mom gives me a gentle squeeze. "My best speeches are always the ones that mean the most to me."

Her phone buzzes. She reads the message and stands up. "I need to go to the West Wing," she says. "But first, I have something for you."

She pulls a small box from her pocket and hands it to me.

"A present?" I ask.

"A souvenir," she says. "From Madagascar."

I open it and gasp.

"A citrine!" I pull the light-yellow crystal from the box. A chain dangles from it.

Before she leaves, Mom fastens the necklace around my neck. I admire it in the mirror.

Maybe it really is some kind of good luck charm. Because now I know what my speech will be about!

CHAPTER 10

Mom and Dad love my idea for my speech: Mom arranges for me to meet an expert to help with my research. Dad sets up a craft space in the Solarium to make my poster. Otto and Ollie even line up their toys to listen to me when I practice!

After school each day, I race home to work on it. At school, I work on it whenever I can. Even during lunch. That also makes it easier to avoid Talia. Because now everything feels weird between us. I'm not pretending anymore. Now, we really aren't talking.

But I do miss her. Especially after I finish writing out the notecards for my speech. I want to show

them to someone. I want to celebrate with someone. But I'm all alone in the library. So I high-five my notebook instead. Which isn't the same.

Finally, the day arrives. I spend the morning keeping my body calm: I remind myself that I can be brave. Because everything will be okay—no matter what happens next. When I realize my heartbeat is getting faster and my stomach is starting to twist, I close my eyes and practice my balloon breathing.

After specials, Miss Jones announces that it's time for my speech. I rush to the front of the class and hang up my poster. Then I turn around and face the class. There are so many people…

There are too many people!

I try looking at just one person, instead. Without realizing it, I look to Talia. But she doesn't look back. She just looks down at her desk with her arms crossed.

Everything I practiced disappears. I forget the reminders that everything will be okay. I forget my balloon breathing. There's only one thing I can think to do.

"Can I go to the restroom first?" I ask.

Cooper groans. "Seriously, Prez? Right *now*?"

Miss Jones nods, and I race out of the classroom. Tony follows and waits outside the restroom. Inside, I lean against the stall door. It's metal and feels cool against my skin. I reach up and touch my new citrine crystal.

I close my eyes. That's when I remember my balloon breathing. I take deep breaths and make sure my belly fills up like a balloon. Then I remind myself that I can be brave and everything will be okay—no matter what happens next. I do it over and over again.

I'm still holding my citrine necklace when I remember: My guidebook said that people used to believe citrine brought them good luck.

That's when I march out of the restroom.

Outside the classroom, Tony whispers, "Good luck."

But I grin and tell him, "Thanks, but I don't need it. I'm ready for this."

He gives me a high-five as I open the door— ready to speak up and give my speech.

Inside, the classroom is almost completely dark.

Only the lights in the front of the room are on. I stand below them and look out into the dark room. I can't really see anyone, which makes it easier to keep my body calm.

I take one more big breath. Then it's time. I start my speech by pointing to my poster: "All About Quartz Crystals."

I describe how quartz is made deep within the earth over thousands of years. I explain how quartz is different from other crystals. I tell them about the Smithsonian and what I learned from the collection manager there. Of course, I also talk about all the different colors of quartz. Then I show them my citrine necklace.

I hear kids whisper, "Ohh." And, "Pretty!"

When I finish, everyone claps. I'm surprised how loud it is. But I'm even more surprised when Miss Jones turns the lights back on.

"Mom!" I shriek when I see her standing in the back of the room. Dad, Rosie and my brothers are there, too. Along with my mom's Secret Service agents. That must have been why the clapping was so loud!

Mom comes to the front of the room. After she

gives me a big hug, she turns to the class.

"Miss Jones and I have arranged a special surprise for all of you."

The class fills with murmurs. Everyone wants to know what the surprise is. Even me!

"We're taking a special field trip to the Smithsonian National Museum of Natural History. We're going to see some quartz in real life!"

"When?" Cooper shouts.

"Right now!" Mom says.

Everyone claps and cheers.

"Really, Mom?" I can't believe it.

"Of course," she says. "I know I'm your mom, but did you forget that I'm also the President?"

We both laugh.

"Come on," she says. "I want to see all the crystals you talked about!"

CHAPTER 11

The kids scramble onto a bus to go to the museum. Of course, Mom and I ride in a Secret Service car.

When we arrive, the bus is already outside the museum's front doors. Kids climb off and form a line into the museum. Then I see Talia. She's not in line with the others. She's on the sidewalk, looking back at the street. I wonder if she's looking for me…

We go in our special entrance and upstairs to the Hall of Geology, Gems and Minerals. Mom goes to the front and talks to the museum's collection manager. It's the same expert I met with for my project. She will lead the class through the exhibit.

I already know all of the information, so I stay at the back of the group. That way, I can take my time.

By the time I get to my favorite quartz display, most of the class is farther ahead. But one student is still there: Talia.

I stop in my tracks, and my body tenses.

But I know what I need to do.

I can't go on pretending I don't see her. I can't go on pretending I don't miss her, either. I take a deep breath and remind myself that I can be brave. Everything will be okay—no matter what happens next. Then, I walk up beside her. It's time for me to speak up about something important.

"I'm sorry I've been avoiding you," I tell her.

Talia looks up at me. I can't tell if she's sad or mad.

"What did I do?" she asks.

I sigh. Part of me wants to say, "Nothing." But I know I need to be brave and speak up to tell her the truth. And remember that everything really will be okay—no matter what happens next.

"I didn't like that you told everyone about my house," I say. "All anyone cared about was what they would eat or order there. That made me sad. And mad...at you for telling them about it."

My hands tremble at my sides. Because I'm not

done yet. "But I should have told you that. I shouldn't have avoided you. I'm sorry for that."

Talia stands still for a moment. Then she bursts into a smile.

"I forgive you!" She throws her arms around my shoulders. "I'm sorry that I told everyone. I just had so much fun! I mean, a flower shop *and* a chocolate shop? *And* a bowling alley? I still can't believe it!"

We both laugh. I have to admit, there are some great things about living in the White House. But then I remember the thing I had wanted to show her there the most.

"I was also sad we didn't get to open the geodes," I whisper.

She stops laughing.

"I'm sorry," she says. "I didn't realize that was so important to you. But I'm glad you told me now."

"Really?" I ask.

"Of course!" she says. "You're my friend, Pippa. How you're feeling matters."

Then, I hear a chuckle behind us. We turn around to see Tony.

"I've been trying to tell her that, too," he says.

This time, we all laugh together.

"Maybe next time, you can come over to my house," Talia says. "I don't have housekeepers or a butler."

Then she grins. "But my dad *is* a chef! And I could finally show you Remington!"

When the tour ends, I say goodbye to Talia. I wait at the entrance with Tony. The kids line up to leave the museum. As they walk by, a lot of them thank me for my speech and the field trip.

Even Cooper stops to say something.

"Prez, this was great," he says.

Like a geode cracking open, I have to speak up about something else...

"Pippa," I announce. I stand up tall and straight.

"What?!" Cooper snorts and shakes his head.

"My name is Pippa." My chest puffs out as I finish explaining. "*Not* Prez."

Cooper scrunches his eyebrows together and is about to say something. Then Dylan jabs him in the side. "Dude!" Dylan points past me as his jaw drops open.

Suddenly, a hand rests on my shoulder. Mom!

"That's right," she says. "I'm the *real* Prez. But you can call me Madam President."

"Uh-uh, okay, M-Madam President," Cooper
stammers. "I-I gotta go!"

I watch as they both scurry away to the bus.

I look up at her. "Thanks, Mom."

"No problem," she says. "I'm proud of you for
speaking up. First with your speech, now with him,
too."

I feel pretty proud of myself, too. Then, I
remember one last thing I need to speak up about.

"Mom, I miss you."

"Oh, Pippa," she says. "I miss you, too. My most

important job is being here for you. Even more than being the President of the United States."

"Really?" I have a hard time thinking *anything* could be more important than that.

"Really," she says. "I'm sorry that I haven't been able to spend much time with you lately. I want to change that."

That's when I get an idea.

"I have some geodes," I say. "I've been saving them for a special occasion. Could we crack them open together sometime?"

"I'd love that." She pulls me in for a hug. "What if you keep one half and I keep the other? I can keep it in the West Wing. Then, whenever I see it, I'll have a little piece of you with me!"

I grin at the thought of my geodes connecting us together.

When the last student exits the museum, Mom grabs my hand. "Ready to get cracking?" Her eyes twinkle like one of my crystals.

"Right now?" I didn't think we'd open the geodes this soon!

"This feels like the perfect special occasion to me," she says with a wink.

Mom laughs and hooks her arm around my shoulders as we walk toward the Secret Service cars.

Maybe having my mom as the President isn't so bad after all!

WHAT DID YOU THINK?!

We would love to know what you thought of Pippa and her story by leaving a review online. Reviews can help other kids find out about Pippa and this book. Make sure to ask your parent first!

Visit www.elizabethjameswrites.com/review or scan this QR code to get links and leave your review:

WHAT CAN YOU SAY IN YOUR REVIEW?

Anything you want! Here are a few things you could share when you write yours:

- What did you like about Pippa?
- What was the most exciting part?
- Did you learn something interesting from Pippa?
- How will this book help you in your own life?
- Are you excited to read the next Pippa book?!

THANKS SO MUCH! You can also share your review on social media and use #PippaPotter so we can find and share it as well!

A GIFT FOR YOU!

As our thanks for reading this book, we've put together a HUGE gift for you!

Whether you're a kid, parent or teacher, our FREE resource guide is jam-packed with activity pages, hand-outs and information sheets to help you explore more about the White House and some of the mental-health strategies mentioned in the book.

This FREE guide includes things like:
- virtual field trips to the White House and Smithsonian Museum
- worksheets for brainstorming your own positive affirmations
- an activity page to help kids discern how their emotions show up in their own bodies
- details about how and why deep breathing works to calm your body down
- instructions for parents and kids to try mindfulness "body scans"
- chapter-by-chapter discussion questions
- and more!

Scan the QR code below or visit www.elizabethjameswrites.com/subscribe to sign up, and we'll send you a link that will give you access to all these resources TODAY!

TOTALLY TRUE!

While Pippa is a make-believe character, there are lots of parts of her story that really are true! For instance, many of the parts about life in the White House and the Smithsonian are based on real facts. Throughout the story, icons like this mark sections that really are true.

Read on to find out which parts in the book are based on facts and learn more about them:

Safety, First! (page 12)

The Secret Service started in 1865. Originally, it provided financial security to the country by stopping people from making fake money. However, in 1901, President McKinley was killed.

That was when the Secret Service became responsible for providing Presidential security, as well. When someone becomes President, everyone in their family receives around-the-clock protection from the Secret Service.

Beauty and the Beast (page 20)

The Secret Service drives a special, super-safe car for the President. It's called "The Beast" because of how safe it is:

Its windows are about five inches thick, so they can't break. It also has special tires that don't deflate even if they get a hole in them. It also can withstand all kinds of dangers, including fire!

The car weighs between 15,000 and 20,000 pounds, and the door is said to be so heavy that a President usually can't open it from inside.

Full House (page 20)

Many Presidents do bring extended family or close friends to live with them in the White House. For instance, President Obama's mother-in-law lived with them while he was in office. With 16 different bedrooms, there's plenty of room there!

Rock On! (page 21)

With more than 350,000 rocks in its collection, the Smithsonian National Museum of Natural History in Washington, D.C., really does have one of the biggest rock collections in the world! Want to check it out for yourself? You can take a virtual tour of the museum when you scan this QR code and sign up for the free *Pippa Speaks Up!* resource guide.

The Wild West (page 22)

The West Wing is in its own separate building to the west of the White House. It is the official workplace of the President and features the Oval Office, the Situation Room, and even a cafeteria called the Navy Mess. It's connected to the White House by the West Colonnade, a long outdoor hallway lined with columns. This colonnade is said to offer Presidents a "45 second commute" to work.

Crack the Code (page 22)

When a President takes office, they really do get

their own code names. The White House Communications Agency picks the President's code name. Then, they assign code names to the rest of the family that usually start with that same letter.

Generally, the names also correspond with their personalities. For instance, President Clinton was called "Eagle," while his wife was called "Evergreen," and his daughter was known as "Energy."

Grand Tour (page 24)

The White House has a long history of being open to the public through tours. These tours take visitors through the downstairs part of the house.

Visitors enter through the East Wing of the White House and can view rooms such as the Family Theater, Library, China Room, Old Family Dining Room and State Dining Room. There is also a Red Room, Blue Room and Green Room on the tour.

The tours are free of charge, but you must submit your request through a member of Congress in advance.

For a virtual tour of the White House, scan the QR code here to get access to the free *Pippa Speaks Up!* resource guide, which includes worksheets, activity pages and more!

SCAN HERE TO GET YOUR FREE RESOURCE GUIDE:

Queen of Clean (page 25)

Can you imagine not having to make your bed or clean your room? If you lived in the White House with a whole team of housekeepers, that could really happen! But just because it could happen doesn't mean it always does.

That was the case for President Obama's daughters: Their parents made them clean their own rooms and make their own beds, without the help of any of the maids.

Like Pippa's parents—and probably yours, too— the Obama's wanted their kids to learn the important skill of "responsibility."

Home Sweet Home (page 25)

The Residence is where the President and their family live, on the second and third floors of the White House. This section is off-limits to visitors.

While almost 1,900 people work throughout the entire White House, about a hundred work solely for the Residence. Jobs include making the President's food, fixing the lights, cleaning and more.

In addition, the Residence is the only part of the White House the First Family can change when they move in. They usually hire a decorator to help and can select furniture and artwork from a special White House collection.

Make Some Room (page 25)

Pippa's room is based off the East Bedroom in the White House, which is also called the Yellow Bedroom. Many former First Kids have lived in this room, including Caroline Kennedy, Tricia Nixon, Susan Ford, Amy Carter, and Chelsea Clinton.

As shown in the illustration on page 26, this room features two sets of shelves that are built into arches in the wall, with a large fireplace between them.

According to the White House Historical Association, the kids cannot make changes to things such as chandeliers, the bed itself or the mirror over the fireplace. However, they can make lots of other changes, including hanging up posters and bringing their own toys and items of interest.

Quartz, Of Course! (page 27)

Quartz is the second most common mineral in the earth's crust. For that reason, it isn't very valuable. However, it does come in different colors.

Those different colors are caused by the addition of heat, radiation or trace minerals. For instance, citrine (the most precious of all quartz gems) gets its color when traces of iron oxide are present. Some other quartz varieties include: amethyst (purple), carnelian (red), onyx (black), and rose quartz (pink).

Lucky Charm (page 27)

Citrine really was believed to bring good luck!

Centuries ago, people thought it would protect them from bad things, bring them wealth and keep them happy. For those reasons, ancient Egyptians, Greeks and Romans used the stone in various ways.

It Takes a Village (page 40)

There are 99 different rooms in the White House basement. It really does have its own carpentry shop, flower shop, chocolate shop, bowling alley —as well as its own dentist's and doctor's offices.

Knowledge is Power (page 41)

Like Doctor Easton told Pippa, it's true that sometimes we don't always realize what we're feeling—especially when we're kids! That's why paying attention to our bodies and how they're feeling is so important.

One way to do that is through doing a "body scan." To try this at home, scan the QR code on the next page to get access to a free *Pippa Speaks Up!* resource guide, which includes complete instructions for parents and kids, as well as other helpful links, worksheets and activity pages.

You're a Gem! (page 45)

The Hall of Geology, Gems and Minerals can be found on the second floor in the Smithsonian National Museum of Natural History.

The Hope Diamond is the most famous item in this collection. It's located at the entrance to the hall. It's bright blue and has attracted more than 200 million visitors over its past 50 years in the museum.

After visitors see the Hope Diamond, they can see more than 7,500 individual gemstones on display. The next section in the Hall looks like an underground mine, where you can learn about different rocks and minerals we use in our everyday lives. The last section in the Hall is all about rocks in space, with one of the largest collections of meteorites in the world.

For a virtual tour of

SCAN HERE FOR YOUR FREE RESOURCE GUIDE:

the Smithsonian's Hall of Geology, Gems and Minerals, scan the QR code on the previous page to get access to a free *Pippa Speaks Up!* resource guide, which includes helpful links, worksheets and activity pages.

Sun Room, Fun Room (page 52)

The Solarium (also called the "Sun Room") was added onto the White House in 1927 by President Coolidge. First Lady Coolidge called it her "sky parlor."

Since then, it has served different uses for different Presidents: It was a playroom for President Franklin Roosevelt's grandchildren; a teen hangout for President Johnson's children (complete with a soda machine!); and a kindergarten classroom for President Kennedy's daughter. (In that setting, it also included a sandbox, just like it does in the story for Pippa's little brothers.)

Presidents without kids have used it for watching television, hosting card games and even grilling out. With large windows overlooking Washington, D.C., it has been a favorite escape for many Presidents.

Going Up! (page 54)

There really are three different elevators in the White House. One is in the Residence. Another is in the pantry. The third is under the Grand Stair in the Entrance Hall. The first elevator was installed in the White House in 1881 by President Arthur.

Perhaps the most famous use of the elevator was when President Theodore Roosevelt's son, Quentin, used it to take a pet pony upstairs to his brother who was sick!

Delicious Dining (page 57)

The White House employs five full-time chefs. They really will make the President whatever they want to eat. For instance, President George W. Bush loved for the chefs to make him "homemade cheeseburger pizza."

All the food is screened before the President ever takes a bite. Plus, the President pays for all the food and meals from their personal account.

Feel Your Feelings (page 69)

Did you know that our bodies can tell us how we are feeling? Researchers have studied it and discovered that different emotions show up in the body in specific ways.

For instance, when someone is feeling anxious or afraid, they can have a twisted feeling in their stomach. Or someone might clench their fists because they're angry. It's important to pay attention to what is going on in our bodies, because sometimes we don't even realize we are feeling a certain way!

Once we pay attention, then we can help our bodies calm down. For an information page about how other emotions show up in our bodies as well as a worksheet to help you notice them in your own body, scan the QR code on the next page below to get access to the free *Pippa Speaks Up!* resource guide.

Breathe Easy (page 71)

Researchers have found that deep, slow breaths really can help your body calm down. For this to happen, though, we have to make sure that we're doing balloon breathing with our bellies. Oftentimes, we breathe only with our chests.

Notice which part of your body fills up when you inhale through your nose: your chest or your belly? When you push your belly out while you inhale, that's balloon breathing. By slowly breathing this way, over and over again, your body can't help but calm down!

Learn more about how and why this works by scanning the QR code below to get access to the free *Pippa Speaks Up!* resource guide.

Pursue the Positive (page 71)

Researchers have also found that positive affirmations can help when you're feeling overwhelmed by fears and other feelings.

Pippa reminds herself, "I can be brave," and, "Everything will be okay—no matter what

SCAN HERE TO
GET YOUR FREE
RESOURCE GUIDE:

happens next." Brainstorm some encouraging things you can tell yourself, or ask a trusted friend or adult to help. Then, make sure to repeat them to yourself, over and over again!

Get access to 10 facts about positive affirmations and worksheets for brainstorming and creating your own by scanning the QR code on the previous page to get access to the free *Pippa Speaks Up!* resource guide.

A World Away (page 73)

Citrine is so rare that it's commonly only found in a few places around the world, including Madagascar. Another place it can be found is in the Ural Mountains in Russia.

However, much of the citrine sold today is actually amethyst, a more common, purple quartz crystal. Shockingly, when amethyst is heated, it turns yellow!

SO MANY THANKS

to the wonderful family, friends and even complete
strangers who helped make this book happen!
I could not have done this without you.

Here are shout-outs to just a few of them.
Special thanks to:

Mom & Dad,
Jenni & Todd,
Rebecca,
Allie & Ellie Abaecherli,
the Lee family,
& the Lutz family
for believing in me and Pippa!

Dr. Brett Dowdy, Dr. Erica Birkley,
Dr. Natalie Thornberry & Katie Dixon
for your professional support!

Claire, Wesley & Gavin
for being kid readers and
sharing your expert opinions for fun!

C.K. Malone, Cassie Silva, Carrie Golus,
A.D. Kemp, April Berry, Lori Keating & Erin Siska
for reading early drafts and offering sharp insights!

Get your **FREE**
RESOURCE GUIDE
for
PARENTS & TEACHERS

A PARENT'S GUIDE TO BODY SCANS WITH KIDS

DISCUSSION QUESTIONS

VISIT THE WHITE HOUSE FROM HOME!

PARENT & TEACHER RESOURCES
to accompany

PIPPA POTTER
PRESIDENT'S DAUGHTER

PIPPA SPEAKS UP!

WRITTEN & ILLUSTRATED BY
ELIZABETH JAMES

SIGN UP TO DOWNLOAD IT NOW:

with more than **25** pages of extra content!

Shop PiPPA POTTER
PRESIDENT'S DAUGHTER
merch

Kids & adult sizes available at:
www.elizabethjameswrites.com/shop

SCAN HERE TO →
VISIT THE SHOP

89089214R00069